'HE CAME, HE SAW, HE CONKED US'!

# ANCIENT ADVENTURES

# AMAZING TALES

Edited By Catherine Cook

First published in Great Britain in 2019 by:

 Young**Writers**

Young Writers
Remus House
Coltsfoot Drive
Peterborough
PE2 9BF
Telephone: 01733 890066
Website: www.youngwriters.co.uk

# FOREWORD

Welcome, Reader!

Are you ready to step back in time? Then come right this way - your time-travelling machine awaits! It's very simple, all you have to do is turn the page and you'll be transported to the past! WOW!

Is it magic? Is it a trick? No! It's all down to the skill and imagination of primary school pupils from around the country. We gave them the task of writing a story about any time in history, and to do it in just 100 words! I think you'll agree they've achieved that brilliantly – this book is jam-packed with exciting and thrilling tales from the past.

These young authors have brought history to life with their stories. This is the power of creativity and it gives us life too! Here at Young Writers we want to pass our love of the written word onto the next generation and what better way to do that than to celebrate their writing by publishing it in a book!

It sets their work free from homework books and notepads and puts it where it deserves to be – out in the world and preserved forever! Each awesome author in this book should be super proud of themselves, and now they've got proof of their imagination, their ideas and their creativity in black and white, to look back on in years to come when their first experience of publication is an ancient adventure itself!

Now I'm off to dive through the timelines and pick some winners – it's going to be difficult to choose, but I'm going to have a lot of fun along the way. I may even learn some new history facts too!

Catherine

# CONTENTS

## Longstone Primary School, Edinburgh

Freddie Knight (8)    44

## Shrewsbury Cathedral Catholic Primary School, Castlefields

Hana Vnoucek (8)    45
Phoenix Daly (9)    46
Oktawian Mioducki    47
Francis David Reavey (9)    48

## Sonning Common Primary School, Sonning Common

Oliver Hughes (11)    49

## St Andrew's Benn CE (VA) Primary School, Rugby

Dewi Harries (11)    50
Joshua Middleton (11)    51
Nicolas Jacko (11)    52

## Vicarage Primary School, East Ham

Habib Abubaker (10)    53
Shasmeen Kuthubudeen (10)    54
Oscar George William Opolot-Oguli (11)    55
Ambreen Aktar (11)    56
Daniella Akosa Osei (12)    57
Eliza Hussain (10)    58
Bilal Ali Raza (9)    59
Zakariya Saeed (11)    60
Nyah Sammy (9)    61
Ifeoma Oti (11)    62
Aneeza Azim (8)    63
Kijorithan Rasikaran (8)    64
Zymal Mobashir Javed (10)    65

Muhammad Yunus Bin-Jamal (10)    66
Rafael Lorenzo Dela Cruz (8)    67
Mushafa Bhatti (10)    68
Amelia Zielinska (8)    69
Zahra Sheeraz (10)    70
Dakshaa Rachana Shourie Mannava (9)    71
Arissa Baloch (10)    72
Madeeha Iffah Hussain (8)    73
Hawwa Khan (10)    74
David Carian (8)    75
Yusuf Hussain (11)    76
Kaydie Laing (9)    77
Orobosa Akenzua (8)    78
Tiffany Paito (9)    79
Josephine Opoku (7)    80
Mehrin Miah (8)    81
Muhammad Yusuf Bin-Jamal (11)    82
Bhagpreet Kaur (10)    83
Sasha Vasudevan (11)    84
Oliver Ronald Otai Opolot-Oguli (9)    85
Muhammad Hasnain Raza (11)    86
Ayaan Zaman (10)    87
Charlotte Cordery (8) & Lottie Cordery (8)    88
Samira Yasmin (9)    89
Hamzah Khan (10)    90
Nafisa Mahmad (9)    91
Kenya Sammy (11)    92
Melissa Rainika (8)    93
Layla Kaur (9)    94
Hannan Khalid (10)    95
Muhammed Zaheer Hussain (10)    96
Yusuf Afnan Hussain (10)    97
Sumayyah Ahmed (10)    98
Dylan Brown (9)    99
Muhammed Zahir Miah (10)    100

| | |
|---|---|
| Shanjai Sritharan (11) | 101 |
| Santhiya Maheswaran (11) | 102 |
| Humayra Islam (11) | 103 |
| Areebah Butt (10) | 104 |
| Linh Pham (8) | 105 |
| Yahya Khan (8) | 106 |
| Yasir Ali (9) | 107 |
| Khadija Hessa Nasim (8) | 108 |
| Muhammad Azeel (9) | 109 |
| Rayan Amjad Ishaq (10) | 110 |
| Joylen Colaco (9) | 111 |
| Anaya Sharma (8) | 112 |
| Shemoli Harrus (10) | 113 |
| Arafathzaman Mohamed | 114 |
| Goda Matuleviciute (8) | 115 |
| Sukhleen Kaur Bains (8) | 116 |
| Nada Hassan (11) | 117 |

## Wilton Primary School, Hawick

| | |
|---|---|
| Ellis Lindores (9) | 118 |
| Sophie Morozzo Della Rocca (10) | 119 |
| Lucas Harry jay Harding (9) | 120 |
| Jenna Quinn (9) | 121 |
| Evie Cranston (10) | 122 |
| Lexi Shiell (10) | 123 |
| Aiva Zoe Barker (9) | 124 |

# THE MINI SAGAS

# The Titantic

Isabella wanted to go on the Titanic but she couldn't afford it. One day, she read something in a shop window about winning a ticket for the Titanic. "It is amazing," she said to her friend. "Let's enter!" So she did.

Two weeks later, Isabella had won a ticket.

A week later and Captain Smith was shouting, "All aboard, welcome everyone."

"Wow, it's so beautiful," said Isabella.

Later on, Isabella heard the crew shouting. "What's going on?"

Then Isabella realised that they'd hit an iceberg.

That night, people were stuck inside. Only the ladies and kids got onto the lifeboats.

**Jasmin Twatt (10)**
Bracoden School, Gamrie

# The Great Battle Of Britain

Meanwhile, in the trench, my pal and I were drinking wine until I heard footsteps everywhere. It was worrying. I heard people whispering, "Oh no, the war is starting again."
So my pal and I went running to the ladder. Suddenly, the captain shouted, "Battle!"
So my pal and I said, sadly at the same time, "Good luck and goodbye."
So off we went to the battle. After a while, the Germans were winning and I was still alive. I killed the last fifty Germans. Everyone roared 'hurrah' and celebrated in the trench.

**Charlie Murray (10)**
Bracoden School, Gamrie

# Last, We See The Stars

"No, Dad! No, Dad! Don't go to the war, you could die and I'll never see you again!"
"Sorry, honey, I have to go and fight for our country and that's that. I leave at dawn."
The night flew past and morning came. By the time I woke up, he was gone.
I waited and waited for a letter to come. Finally, one came and this is what it said: 'Dear Lilly, I have landed in France and I'm getting ready for war. Hope you're getting on okay at home. Yours, Dad'.
After that letter, I never saw him again.

**Aleisha Ritchie (10)**
Bracoden School, Gamrie

# Beyond The Bars Of Auschwitz

'Sister, death is our destiny behind the bars that separate our freedom...' wrote Gal in his letter to his beloved sister, Golda. His heart was anguished with grief. He knew they all had a look of hunger and willing in their eyes.

Just then, his mind took him back to his best friend, shot in front of his innocent eyes. He'd never forget that moment when a life was taken from one who was close to his heart.

Suddenly, Gal heard shouting from the train tracks. He saw Golda. Tears ran down his cheeks, she would never read his letter.

**Rosa Henderson (11)**
Bracoden School, Gamrie

# The Christmas Truce - The Great War

The wind blew, the snow fell softly. Silence was in the air on Christmas Day. Britain was singing. The Germans joined in. Scott was the brave one, he got out of the trench and surrendered. Then a German, who was called Bob, climbed out of the trench too. Then it happened. Everyone got out of the trenches and they were shaking hands. They were taking pictures of each other.

Then a football was thrown out of the trench. The score was 3-2 to Germany. Then the fun was over and they had to go back into the trenches and fight.

**Joel Wiseman (11)**
Bracoden School, Gamrie

# The War Raid

It'd been a year since World War One had started and it had been nothing but trouble. One British soldier, Dave, decided to venture over to the German side. "I'll rob them whether they like it or not," he said to himself proudly.

When he made it, he saw the first thing he could rob, a tank! He saw that it was locked, so he knew the key was in the trenches. He went into the trenches to find it. He saw it but it was being guarded by soldiers. He went and defeated everyone, then he took the key.

**James Leslie Hewett (10)**
Bracoden School, Gamrie

# Life In The Trenches

Bombs went off. All I could hear was *boom, boom, boom!* You could see the bullets flashing past. The Germans were advancing towards me and my friends. It was the battle of Ypres. We could see our comrades falling as the enemy advances towards the Western Front and the British Army. Our trench was filled with corpses and rats the size of cats. Some were the size of dogs and ate from corpses. They were pushing us back to the reserve trenches for safety but we will have hope. The Germans had run out of supplies and surrendered.

**Ciaran Andrew Brown (10)**
Corpus Christi Primary School, Glasgow

# The Past Is A Blast!

I was in my super cool time machine. I was flicking switches and pressing buttons. I went to the past! *Bang! Crash! Thump!* I arrived. Now the fun could start. First, I went to 1717 and sailed the seas with Blackbeard. Next, I travelled to 1848 to have tea with Queen Victoria. Then I travelled eighty-two million years back and rode a dinosaur. My next stop was 1606 and there I helped Shakespeare write Macbeth. Next, I wrapped a mummy in ancient Egypt. At last, I went back to the present and realised I had changed history!

**Megan Brown (10)**
Corpus Christi Primary School, Glasgow

# The Bite

One hot day in Egypt, Cleopatra was walking to the market. She walked around the shops and saw this gem. She said, "That gem is the most beautiful thing."
So the princess went to the shop and bought the gem.
On the way home, the gem started to speak. It flicked up a map and Cleopatra said, "Let's go, I can't wait."
First, she went home and put her shopping things away. The gem led her to a dark place and the princess quivered. She kept walking, when all of a sudden, "Help! Aarghh!"
She was bitten...

**Olivia Leask (10)**
Darnley Primary School, Glasgow

# The World War One Disaster

I woke up to see bombs dropping and people dying. I was getting used to it because we'd been here for two months. War took a long time to finish. Something changed, a man from the opposite army came up without guns but his hands in the air. I couldn't believe he'd surrendered.

After that, we became friends. Sadly, one of my mates dropped a bomb by accident and nearly everyone died. Luckily, I survived but I had a very bad injury on my leg and arm. I'd broken my arm and my legs, had lots of cuts and bruises.

**Hafsa Muhammad (10)**
Darnley Primary School, Glasgow

# Battle Of The Martians

In 1914, a light came on us. A big, glowing ball of light. I watched as it flew over and crashed into a hillside. A massive creature came crawling out of the meteor. I watched as it walked towards us. I was terrified as it walked closer and closer. My heart was pounding. We fought as it sent out ribbons and strangled my comrade to death. My comrades were all dead. The Martian went over the trench. Sometime after, a group of British came and I couldn't fight back. I was outnumbered. I decided to surrender to the British.

**Ivan He (9)**
Darnley Primary School, Glasgow

# The Adventure Of Rome

One day a boy called Ross and a girl called Rebecca were digging in the garden and they found a coin. They thought it was just a coin but it was an ancient coin from Rome. So they rubbed it to clean it and then they went back in time to Rome. So they started their adventure.

They came across a villa and in the villa, there was a big courtyard. They wandered in and it was all quiet until a voice said, "Who are you? What are you doing?"

"Nothing..." replied Rebecca.

**Poppy Whitelock (9)**
Darnley Primary School, Glasgow

# The Jungle

Ava and Carys went on an adventure. They went to the woods and somehow, they found a dinosaur footprint. They were sort of lost. So Carys went into her bag to get her phone and it said it was the dinosaur times. They weren't lost in a wood, they had time travelled back in time.

They came across a raptor and a T-rex, so they ran as fast as they could. All they could hear was roaring. They tripped and fell into a hole. They ended up back in their woods.

**Aimee Elizabeth Howson (10)**
Darnley Primary School, Glasgow

# Lost Holiday

My friends and I were going on a plane to Florida. When we got there, we went to explore. We went through the woods and found something shining. It was a golden cup. It was dusty and I had to rub it to see what it said. As soon as I rubbed it, we went to a whole new place. I was quite smart, so I knew where we were... Rome. We went to the bathhouse. We got a nice massage. Then we wanted to go back home, so I rubbed the cup and we were back.

**Ruby Cavangh (10)**
Darnley Primary School, Glasgow

# The Plague! The First And Only Adventure

Dear Diary,
I started my day by seeing someone die of the plague. My heart started to pound and I tried to fight it off but it will do no good. I still have a couple of days left.

Dear Diary,
It's the next day, I don't know if I will live. I can barely speak.

Dear Diary,
Hello, I am the wife of William. Unfortunately, he died of hunger. This is his diary.

**Caleb Wilkie (10)**
Darnley Primary School, Glasgow

# A Day In The Trench

On a cold and windy day, two little girls walked through a trench. Their names were Anastasia and Isabella. They really liked each other. Walking through the muddy field, their shoes were getting stuck in the squishy mud and smelly trenches. They couldn't believe what they could hear, only gunshots. They wanted to go home...
Then they woke up, it was just a dream.

**Ava McChristie (10)**
Darnley Primary School, Glasgow

# The Battle Of Friendship

As the sun came up over our gladiator school, we got up, had breakfast and started training. Today I had to battle my friend Tiberius, so then I was escorted to the gate.

It opened and I walked out. Tiberius said, "Good luck," and I said it back. We started to battle and he surrendered to me.

Emperor Nero said to kill but I fired an arrow at him. He didn't die, so we ran out into town and battled some guards. Then we were free.

We ran to a tree hut and lived in it and we're free forever.

**Ryan Hopkins (10)**
Deighton Primary School, Tredegar

# The Fight Of Perseus And Hades

In the kingdom, there was an evil god called Hades. He was evil and tried to attack Zeus but Zeus saw it coming and banished him to Hell. Danae was told that the god Zeus looked down from Olympus and fell in love. Zeus came down and married Danae, they had a son called Perseus. Hades escaped from Hell using his hell hounds. Perseus grew up fast and was given a sword. Hades found them in a village and attacked Perseus because it was a way to get revenge against Zeus. Perseus used his sword to stab Hades' heart.

**Finley Mackintosh (10)**
Deighton Primary School, Tredegar

# Gods Go To The Human World

Gods and gladiators were once interested in what the human world would be like if they went there. So they went to the human world and started to eat their food, their drinks and even started wearing their clothes. But only the gods went, not the gladiators. Zeus recommended a potion that turned them into humans. They even made a potion that turned them back to a human body again, so now they could go. Then they were happily small, like a human. There wasn't any fear from the humans but they were still the gods.

**Rosie Phillips (8)**
Deighton Primary School, Tredegar

# The Escape

Rome was a place where gladiators fought and some were locked up. One day, all the slaves escaped. The slaves took down the guards and started pretending to be taken away. The slaves were smart but not smart enough. The boss knew all of the guards and the slaves weren't any of them. The boss sent the rest of the guards to capture them, but the slaves ran as fast as they could. Their hearts were beating and their palms were sweaty. Finally, the slaves were out. "Freedom!" shouted Spartacus.

**Louie Ray Tyler (10)**
Deighton Primary School, Tredegar

# The Viking's Defeat

There once lived a boy who loved scuba diving. The boy was called Tom. Tom had heard that his island was getting taken over and it was true. Tom's family and friends were all taken and Tom tried to search for them.

Tom had grabbed his uncle's sword from the drawer and went onto the Viking boat. Tom started to kill all of the Vikings and freed all of his friends and family. He gave all of them swords. They defeated every one of the Vikings and hit the Viking captain off the boat. Tom was proud.

**Cameron Pope (9)**
Deighton Primary School, Tredegar

# Angel At The Graveyard

A grave fell, the sound echoing as the girl entered the graveyard. Then she went to sit down by her nan's grave. Her nan had been the queen, so she'd been wrapped up like a mummy. So she sat down by the grave and sat there for a while, wishing she could still be alive. Then she heard a bang and a mummy entered the graveyard. Her jaw dropped and she ran as fast as she could but there wasn't a way out. She sucked her lip as the mummy circled her. She soon found that there were angels dancing...

**Summer Grace Williams (9)**
Deighton Primary School, Tredegar

# Perseus And The Medasu

I ran and I could hear the wind behind me and hissing from the snakes. I grabbed my sharp, silver sword and ran into the deep, damp forest. Medusa hissed, she turned to the tree that I was hiding behind. My heart stopped and my jaw dropped. Cleverly, I grabbed my shield to use it as a mirror to see Medusa's reflection. She turned her back to me and walked off. I sneaked up behind her and swung my sword into her neck. Blood gushed out like a water fountain. This part of my task was done.

**Tynisha K (10)**
Deighton Primary School, Tredegar

# The Minotaur

*Thump. Thump.* Closer and closer, the beast came quickly, charging fast. I slipped and saw a smooth, pointy horn but I didn't know for sure if it was his. Saliva dribbled to the ground. I saw his skin, black as night. I grabbed my sword and quickly dashed to a tree. The creature charged again. I lifted my shield, jumped and swiped my sword. *Thud!* Something dropped to the floor. I realised what it was. I picked it up and I was holding the Minotaur's horn.

**Noah Pearsall (9)**
Deighton Primary School, Tredegar

# The Quest For The Mummy's Pyramid

Once there was a mummy that lived in Egypt. People were scared of him but one was brave enough to find the mummy that was in a pyramid. It was a long time before he got into the pyramid, so he went back home.

The next day, he got into the pyramid. If he did it wrong, he would get burnt or even die. So the man was cautious. Then he saw the mummy and he grabbed it. It knocked him out and brought him back. The mummy wrapped him up and he became the mummy's friend.

**Rio-Jai Duggan (10)**
Deighton Primary School, Tredegar

# Perseus

There was once a slave known as Perseus, he was one of the best there was. Perseus was a slave for years and he got fed up. He got all of the slaves into an army and he sent his men to the kitchen to gather as many knives as possible. He saw some guards, so he led his slave army to a gigantic wall. He collected vines and got up there by using the vines. Then they got down and they almost defeated Rome but they all died in battle.

**Cole Pikulski (9)**
Deighton Primary School, Tredegar

# The Titanic

One night, I heard a horrific sound. Water gushed through the hallways. What was happening? My brain froze like the icy water around me. Suddenly, water leaked into the ship faster and faster. Everyone evacuated to the top of the Titanic. The captain pulled the yellow boats up to the deck. Women had to go first with their babies.

It was my turn... I climbed in. We got lowered to the sea and we started paddling. The men pushed to get to the front. Soon everyone safely moved onto the boats. Many people died that day. I was devastated.

**Matilda Lipscombe (9)**
Greenmount Primary School, Ryde

# The Planes Come Over London!

One afternoon, in London, all the sky became dark. Suddenly, there was a loud bang and it came from the distance. The whole of London went silent and lots of planes came over, turning the sky black. Everyone in London rushed to their bomb shelters thinking, *safety first!* Something was attacking and they found out it was Germany, they were attacking France.

We didn't know what to do, so we sent over our men to fight. At one point, they got stuck on the beach because they got pushed, so they sent over boats to rescue the men.

**Sadie Tottman (9)**
Greenmount Primary School, Ryde

# Dino Neighbours

One time there were two dinosaurs, they never liked each other at all. They lived opposite each other.

A few months went past and then they thought they needed to fight. So they ran out to each other, *clash, scratch, scrape!* Red sticky blood came pouring out of each of them. Tumbling, rumbling and crashing with their razor-sharp teeth, they got bites to the neck, breaking bones, bleeding noses and scratches to the eyeballs. They ran and ran back home but then there was a crackling noise. It was the two suns, it was a meteorite!

**Roscoe John Lloyd (9)**
Greenmount Primary School, Ryde

# The Titanic

One dark night, everyone entered a big ship called the Titanic. Everyone sat and children ran around. I sat down and chatted to Oliver. He was a very good train driver and we were chatting about a threatening wave that was crashing onto the side of the ship.

There was a gigantic iceberg in the middle of the ocean. As the ship approached it, everyone got to one side and screamed. We hit the iceberg and everyone slid off into the freezing cold water. Oliver drowned but I was caught by a boat called the Isle of Wight Rescue Service.

**Leo Thomas-Smith (9)**
Greenmount Primary School, Ryde

# Boudica The Great

A blood-splattered sword swished through the muggy air, slashing down on a Roman's face. It knocked his helmet askew and I took my chance, seizing his helmet I yanked it off and slashed his nose. A stream of dark-red blood soaked us both. I stood drenched in it, watching the chaos on the battlefield. Half of the Romans lay like the one at my feet, dead. I watched my warriors yelling my name as they ran at the fighters.

A Roman charged at me, he had no helmet on as I pounced, cutting across his eye. Then he fell, dead.

**Jaime Wade (9)**
Greenmount Primary School, Ryde

# The Discovery Of Tutankhamun

In a city called Cairo, a man called Howard Carter was trying to find a tomb. He was digging, when all of a sudden, he spotted a glimpse of gold. He dug some more until he could step through the gap. As soon as he stepped through, he saw an amazing room full to the brim with gold and silver. As he stepped forward, he saw an amazing sarcophagus. He lifted the lid, the mummy spoke these words, "How dare you disturb the Pharaoh of Egypt!" Then it went to sleep again. Howard died five years later, he was cursed!

**Mary Ann Roper (9)**
Greenmount Primary School, Ryde

# The Book Of The Dead

I was waiting outside the door of the room where my heart would be weighed. I heard them shout my name and I entered. Covering the walls were spells of some sort of painted hieroglyphs. I turned into a hawk and flew on the tomb and watched as they weighed my heart against the feather. Anubis, the jackal-headed god, weighed them and my heart was lighter.

Thoth, the baboon, made sure it was weighed fair and it was! Horus wrote spells on the walls and then took me through. I had my meal and I went to the afterlife.

**Jacob Williams (9)**
Greenmount Primary School, Ryde

# Tutu's Escape

Tutu was married to somebody called Ani. As Tutu walked with him, she leant down with a small rattle. Ani was really scared because he was about to get his heart weighed. As he entered the Hall of Truth, he could feel death around him. Anubis weighed the heart. On top of the scales was a magic bird to make sure there was no cheating. Then something happened, his heart was heavy. He got up and ran out, then he heard something behind him and it was the gobbler. It clutched its fist and bit their tongue. Tutu escaped.

**Lillie-Mae Elizabeth Flesher (9)**
Greenmount Primary School, Ryde

# The Book Of The Dead

Before I entered the tomb my heart was racing. As I entered the room I saw an unimaginable creature. Too scared to speak, I bowed my head. Thoughts raced through my mind, *have I been good enough? What if I've been bad and have a bad heart? What will happen?* Suddenly, I remembered it would be eaten by Ammute, the gobbler.

Watching the weighing was tense. As the judges watched and weighed my heart, I've never felt tenser but I was relieved that my heart was lighter than a feather.

**Noah Rodenby (9)**
Greenmount Primary School, Ryde

# The Book Of The Dead

I walked into the Hall of Truth trying to get to the afterlife. I said goodbye to Tutu, then walked in. I was very scared. Tutu had died long before me. Tutu was a high priestess with a musical instrument in her hand. I was a scribe. The heart was weighed against the feather to see if the heart was lighter. Anubis weighed the heart, he was half jackal and half human. On top of the scales sat Horus, making sure it was done properly. Horus was counting spells to help me through to the afterlife.

**Alfie Hanson (9)**
Greenmount Primary School, Ryde

# Julius Caesar Wants A Pizza

One day, Julius Caesar said, "I want a pizza."
The servants didn't know what a pizza was, they said, "But sir, what is a pizza?"
"I don't know," Julius said, "but get me one."
So the servants looked everywhere for a pizza; they checked the market place, the colosseum and they probably checked nearly all of Rome. They couldn't find a pizza, so they returned to the palace and said, "Sir, we couldn't find a pizza..."
They stopped as a person called, "Pizzas! Pizzas! Get your pizzas here."
The servants and Julius ran out to the cart and ate pizzas.

**Louie Kieran (10)**
Holy Rosary Primary School, Belfast

# Adventures Of Egypt

Once, Alec was walking through the dark pyramid. According to the map, he was reaching the middle of the pyramid. He saw the treasure. He ran over and grabbed it. A loud rumbling filled the chamber. Suddenly, rocks began to fall. Alec ran as fast as he could. A loud voice said, "Alec, you have taken my treasure. Now you will pay..."

Alec was frightened and sped up. He could see the exit straight ahead. Small creatures began appearing, flying all over the place. The exit was closing. Alec rolled out and the door shut. Finally, it was all over.

**Aidan William Kee (10)**
Holy Rosary Primary School, Belfast

# Freya

Freya's a young, beautiful goddess of love. One day, Freya decided to go on a walk but it started to rain, so she hid in a cave. She went further into the cave and then she started hearing noises, so she wanted to check it. There were seven goblins. They were digging gold. She asked them for a necklace and they gave her one but in return, they wanted a kiss each. Everyone noticed the necklace. They told her to return it to the goblins and if she didn't, they'd punish her. So the next day, Freya returned the necklace.

**Gaja Wolniewicz (11)**
Holy Rosary Primary School, Belfast

# Thor And Loki

Thor and Loki were out walking in the grounds of Asgard. Suddenly, a loud noise shook the ground, a large crack opened up in the marble floor. A horde of about five hundred giants crawled out. Thor stuck out his hand and summoned his hammer. Loki turned into a bird and flew at the giants. Thor swung his hammer at the giants and knocked down about three hundred with one blast. Loki flew around, pecking the giants as he flew around them. The giants became scared and fled. Thor ran over to Loki and finally, the fighting was over.

**Mitchell Stuart (10)**
Holy Rosary Primary School, Belfast

# The Curse Of King Tutankhamun

A group of Egyptologists went to find King Tutankhamun's tomb. After a long time of searching, they found it. It was the only tomb that was completely intact. It was said that whoever enters the tomb will be cursed. One of the men had heard of this curse and didn't go in but the rest thought he was foolish. They stole the valuables and left.

Later that week, one of the men died of a heart attack which was strange because he was extremely healthy. The rest died except for one, the one who hadn't gone in!

**Geri Mallon (10)**
Holy Rosary Primary School, Belfast

# The Missing Fellow

Thor and Loki were in Asgard, doing casual things. Then Thor saw two goblins charging towards them. When the goblins came, they threw powder into Thor's eyes and he was blinded. He finally got the powder out but he couldn't find Loki. So he set off on a quest to find Loki and he went to Midgard. Thor kept exploring and then he found a cave but he didn't want to go in it. He checked everywhere, bushes, trees and lakes but couldn't find Loki. Then Thor lost hope, he couldn't find Loki...

**Dachi Kekelishvili (10)**
Holy Rosary Primary School, Belfast

# The Ambush

One day in Asgard, a letter, all the way from Jotunheim, had arrived. It was from the King of Giants and mentioned that Odin had to come to Jotunheim and have a duel with the king. If Odin didn't come, then he was a coward. So Odin accepted the challenge and arrived at the castle where the giants lived. However, when he entered, the men appeared from nowhere and punched him and he fainted.

When he woke up, he noticed that he had been ambushed by the giants. He escaped and now he was at war.

**Anayraj Tripathi (10)**
Holy Rosary Primary School, Belfast

# Egyptian Gods

It was a sunny day in ancient Egypt, the Romans were invading. Cleopatra was in her temple of Egyptian gods, she was begging to the gods to get the Romans away. The gods agreed to help her. As the Romans were about to enter the kingdom, a big cloud came over the Nile and a mist came down so none of the Romans could see where they were going. Then Cleopatra's army attacked the Romans and they fled in terror as they thought the guards were Egypt's ghosts.

Cleopatra thanked the gods for their help in saving the Egyptian kingdom.

**Freddie Knight (8)**
Longstone Primary School, Edinburgh

# The Menacing Mummy And The Sabotaging Sphinx

The wind howled, my heart was racing so fast as the menacing mummy and the sabotaging sphinx chased me through Egypt, where the ancient Egyptians lived. Through the valleys, through the pyramids, through the rushes of the Nile river, this journey was vital to get through. The sphinx and mummy barged forwards, trying to catch up. Ahead of them, I tripped up over a rock. As they caught up, I tore the bandages off the mummy. Screaming, I cried, "Mum, Mum! Where are you?"
My mum came rushing and said, "Don't worry, it was all a bad dream, darling!"

**Hana Vnoucek (8)**
Shrewsbury Cathedral Catholic Primary School, Castlefields

# Where's My Mummy?

Once upon a time, there were two tomb robbers called James and John. They were going to the pharaoh's tomb to steal his riches so they could sell them. They went in and saw the lights were turned off. They carried on walking through the tomb to find the pharaoh's riches when they saw an old picture of Ra, an Egyptian god. The robbers took the picture and held it. Then they heard a coin drop, so they went to where they'd heard the coin. They noticed that a person was standing. It was a mummy, they ran away forever.

**Phoenix Daly (9)**
Shrewsbury Cathedral Catholic Primary School, Castlefields

# The Bloodthirsty Battle

Octavian Augustus was the first Roman emperor. I heard that on TV. I was named after him because he was a genius and a great politician. He was also scared of thunder and lightning, just like me! Or maybe because I'm fighting with my brother just like he did with Marcus Antonius.

One day me and my brother were battling. I didn't have a real army but that didn't stop me. The bloodthirsty battle took place in our kitchen. When we finished, ketchup-blood was everywhere and I got a mop as my trophy.

**Oktawian Mioducki**
Shrewsbury Cathedral Catholic Primary School, Castlefields

# The Two Chimney Sweepers And Their Bad Master

I am in an old house, doing nothing except cleaning chimneys with my brother, George. George and I want to escape and we have many times, well, at least tried to. We are going to try and escape today and I hope it works.

I made a scene when George was ready. We ran but Sir Albert was right behind us. We went through a tunnel but we came to Buckingham Palace. Queen Victoria was outside and was telling us to stop. I hope she'd punish him. She did but she also took us as well. We had a happy life.

**Francis David Reavey (9)**
Shrewsbury Cathedral Catholic Primary School, Castlefields

# Gunshots On Doomsday

My heart stopped when I saw all the enemies on the D-Day beach. I hoped I could get through this doomsday. Then suddenly, our boat hit the beach and the hatch opened.

My friends, Ben and Jake, and I ran onto the beach. After a few seconds, we were already under fire. We all ran to a rock to protect ourselves while the turret shot at us. The turret stopped firing to save ammunition but my friend Jake thought it had run out of ammunition and tried to run. He was shot dead in seconds...

**Oliver Hughes (11)**
Sonning Common Primary School, Sonning Common

# The Plot

It is the year 1605, I am Sir George Sargetron. I am a guard of King James the first. Recently, we've had a note from an unknown person that there will be something interesting happening on November 5th. Currently, I'm walking with other Beefeaters to the Houses of Parliament to investigate. There is a man!
"Stop right there, sir. Explain why you're under Parliament with multiple barrels of gunpowder?" yelled one fo the beefeaters.
"You're under arrest for attempting to explode Parliament," said a guard.

**Dewi Harries (11)**
St Andrew's Benn CE (VA) Primary School, Rugby

# The Monster From The Cave!

The wind howled and sand blew up into the ice-cold chilly air. Apart from the howling of the wind, the desert was silent and desolate. I cowered in fear as sand brushed past my frozen pale cheeks. From the corner of my eye I spotted a small cave. Interested by what I saw I forced my legs to edge forward towards it. The entrance was guarded by a boulder. I was petrified. In front of me a red-eyed Minotaur stood. It looked hungry, its breath smelt stale. I was doomed! The last I heard was, "Hello," before the inevitable.

**Joshua Middleton (11)**
St Andrew's Benn CE (VA) Primary School, Rugby

# The Mystery Of The Mummies

It was a boiling hot day in Egypt. The king heard some weird noises while walking around the pyramids. He was a bit frightened to walk inside but he did walk inside. There were lots of shadows moving.

When the king took a further two steps, all was black. There was a bright light of shining gold. Inside were a pair of mummies, his heart froze. He had one thing on his mind, no, it wasn't stealing gold, it was to run. The pyramid was shaking, there was a roar from the front and mummies behind him. He was trapped.

**Nicolas Jacko (11)**
St Andrew's Benn CE (VA) Primary School, Rugby

# The Falling Out

"What?" Hercules asked.

"That's right, we aren't apologising!" Agamemnon responded.

"But other men are sick, dying even," Hercules replied.

"'Our men'? You mean, *my* men? You may have significance, Hercules, but these are my men and I am the leader!" Agamemnon claimed.

"Your pride is more important than the men's lives then, huh? Their families, forget them, their hopes and dreams, dump 'em because your pride is more important than their lives. This can't and won't involve me any longer," Hercules argued.

And off he went. Hercules stayed true to his word and left Agamemnon and his men.

**Habib Abubaker (10)**
Vicarage Primary School, East Ham

# Confucius And Confused Chen

Deep in ancient China, there lived an enlightened (but very perplexing) man who always gave quotes to his people. Not many of the people understood what he actually meant. One person was allowed to ask a question for each quote.

Confucius bellowed, "Baseball is wrong - a man with four balls cannot walk!"

When Confucius said the quote, a hand went up.

"What do you mean?" said Chen, a citizen.

"I mean, Baseball is wrong - a man with four balls cannot walk!" Confucius bawled.

"Yeah, but what do you mean?" shrieked Chen.

"That's it, out!"

And Confucius stormed out.

**Shasmeen Kuthubudeen (10)**
Vicarage Primary School, East Ham

# The Blitz

*Boom!* Babies were screaming. *Bang!* Newly built houses had been destroyed and sirens were booming.

"Everyone, get to the train stations, the Germans are here!" Winston Churchhill demanded.

Mothers and fathers kept a firm grip on their children as they scurried and scuttled to the hideouts. Debris fell from buildings like rain, houses crumbling onto the road as people sprinted for their lives. I thought it was a demolition site.

As I ran, I heard blood-curdling shrieks. Suddenly, fire engulfed the town and I was scared, terrified and horrified. I was surrounded by flames when I spotted a bucket...

**Oscar George William Opolot-Oguli (11)**
Vicarage Primary School, East Ham

# They're Here!

The wind whistled while screams enveloped the village. There was nowhere to run and nowhere to hide. Orangey-yellow flames were dancing wildly, conquering another hut and another life. Swords viciously swung at frightened silhouettes cowering in fear. Bloodied axes in pale bodies.

The young girl shuddered with shock and fear. *Why is this happening?* Vikings had arrived, armoured with strong steel helmets and metal chest plates, ready to invade and destroy happiness. Monks were killed and forced to be slaves because of their religious beliefs. Their cold-blooded minds were overfilling with anger as they turned to the girl...

**Ambreen Aktar (11)**
Vicarage Primary School, East Ham

# The Spinner

Long ago in ancient Greece, there was once a gifted weaver called Arachne. As proud as she was, she challenged the Goddess Athena to see who was the better weaver. Athena accepted the friendly challenge and decided to weave a warning so that Arachne realised her mistake - challenging a Greek goddess! Not realising the danger she was in, Arachne wove four beautiful, intricate scenes. To make matters worse, Arachne's work didn't show the gods in a favourable light. Humiliated and angry, Athena cursed Arachne and transformed her into an eight-legged creature.

Maybe that's why spiders are constantly spinning webs?

**Daniella Akosa Osei (12)**
Vicarage Primary School, East Ham

# The Mummy And The Ancient Desert

One day Amy and Bob were going for a walk in the ancient desert. Then they saw an ancient pyramid. They went inside the ancient pyramid.

"What is this?" said Amy.

"It's a mummy," said Bob. "What's this?"

"It's some type of writing," said Amy.

Bob read it out and some magic started to come out.

"What have you done?" screamed Amy.

They hid under the table. The next minute, a mummy came alive.

"Can you see what I can see?" whispered Bob.

"Yes," replied Amy.

The mummy found them and it was the end of their lives.

**Eliza Hussain (10)**
Vicarage Primary School, East Ham

# Victorian Troubles

"Come on, John, you're walking far too slowly," I exclaimed, as I trudged despondently, desperately looking for a refuge.

John was getting colder and colder and weaker and weaker as the seconds passed. As the cloudless moonlight shone on a sign quoting *Dr Barnado: Care Home for Girls and Boys.* I knocked on the bulky black doors. *Knock, knock.* A smart looking, rich and well-dressed woman approached me with a voice as kind as an angel.

"Has Dr Barnardo called you here? Are you Hannah and John?" she asked, looking at her papers.

"Yes, miss," I replied nervously.

**Bilal Ali Raza (9)**
Vicarage Primary School, East Ham

# The Blitz

It was raining bullets in the trenches. Bullets were penetrating rapidly which had left me soaked in my neighbour's blood. Thousands of young men had been fooled into joining the army and died, like me. So as I left the bath of blood, in the distance a subtle object zoomed across the sky, it was a plane. Many planes. They all had decelerated and then dropped bombs over London. *Boom! Crash! Bang!* Bombs were dropping faster than raindrops. London was flooded with innocent people's blood. Decades later, this terrible incident was remarked as the Blitzkrieg - the lightning war.

**Zakariya Saeed (11)**
Vicarage Primary School, East Ham

# Mummy Busters

Long, long ago, a mummifier wanted to show his wife that being a mummifier is good and that his daughter should be one. So the wife said, "Let's go to the tomb and see if she likes it, okay?"
"Okay," he replied.
So they went to the tomb. As they arrived, they stepped in and the door shut behind them. "Are you sure this isn't a haunted room?"
"Oh no, that's just a myth."
"It'll be quick."
So they took some keys and looked around. They felt like they were being watched. They turned around and saw a mummy!

**Nyah Sammy (9)**
Vicarage Primary School, East Ham

# Nowhere To Go!

Swords and axes swung round Fay as she dodged for her life. She didn't know what to do. The vicious creatures' silhouettes were everywhere and their boats surrounded the country like big bullies. Peeking over the table that she was hiding behind, she noticed a muscular figure. The chase continued. The horrified girl's beautiful hair flew in the wind.

Fay was now in the wilderness and hopefully no longer at the edge of death. Scuttling around in the bushes, she heard a noise. Full of fright, she crawled across the soft grass. What was that thing she had just heard...?

**Ifeoma Oti (11)**
Vicarage Primary School, East Ham

# The Haunted Hosptal

In winter as cold as ice, there lay a village where a young girl called Florence Nightingale's dream was to be a nurse. However, her parents didn't like it when she helped out.

"Florence, why are you working?" he would say.

"Daddy, I like it!" Florence shouted.

Her dad gasped like a fish.

As she grew, she got a job as a nurse. She went to Scutari in the pitch-black night. When the wind howled, and the trees cowered, Florence found a part of the hospital was covered in rats. She screamed for help loudly. She didn't go back there.

**Aneeza Azim (8)**
Vicarage Primary School, East Ham

# The Death Of Cavemen

"Aarghh!" yelled the funny, cowardly caveman. He was running from billions of predators. The coward's name was Cheddar Man. He never slept. He lived in a cave where insects lived. Every night he arrived with a dead animal. He would cook the food and feed his family.

When Cheddar Man went out hunting, within a blink of an eye, he spotted a giant, bloody, stinky mammoth and he ran off as fast as a cheetah with his spear.

"You shall never live!" yelled Cheddar Man angrily. Then the evil mammoth poked the man and made him choke blood out monstrously.

**Kijorithan Rasikaran (8)**
Vicarage Primary School, East Ham

# Beware! The Killer Is Coming!

It's coming closer and closer, my wedding with the handsome king but something has cautioned me. *Beware, the killer is here! The killer is here, much closer to you.* I thought it was nothing.

After the marriage, I got pregnant. Hurray! But I was worried because my husband said he *needed* a son or there would be consequences. Then something said, "Don't upset the killer or you will be like the first wife! The one who gave birth to a girl, Mary."

I then soon faced the consequences of upsetting him. The killer was Henry VIII. I was dead...

**Zymal Mobashir Javed (10)**
Vicarage Primary School, East Ham

# Unfortunate Events WW2

Many years ago, life wasn't easy for the three unfortunate children because their father had been kidnapped in war. They were in search of their missing father but there wasn't any news of him until one mysterious day, a crooked man knocked on the door. Then they heard the terrible news, he had been killed.

The three miserable children were in tears, they couldn't believe what had happened. They didn't believe him and the man said, "Come to this deserted place to see the dead body."

So the children left but little did they know, it was a trap.

**Muhammad Yunus Bin-Jamal (10)**
Vicarage Primary School, East Ham

# The Chase Of The Mummy

It was a peaceful, hot day in the scorching desert of ancient Egypt. The pharaoh died and the people were voting for their next king. Suddenly, there was a giant rumble coming from the pyramid and something weird came out from the smoke... it was a mummy!
Everyone panicked and screamed. Every second it grew larger and larger until it grew to the height of the Empire State Building. People evacuated on ships but they were destroyed. People were making armies of swords and they climbed the Titan. Finally, they won. Everyone cheered and rejoiced as they started voting again.

**Rafael Lorenzo Dela Cruz (8)**
Vicarage Primary School, East Ham

# The Game Of Egyptians

Once upon a time in America, there was a perplexing war going on in New York City in 2000 BC.

"Run!" said the elder sister. "There's a war going on!"

The three siblings were running and the younger one fell down. Then they saw a substantial hole. They went in it but when they were in the middle of the hole, they saw a gigantic mummy-faced Egyptian door. They went in it and as they did, everything altered. Everything disappeared. All they saw was sand.

"We're in Egypt!" said the middle sibling. "Now what do we do?"

**Mushafa Bhatti (10)**
Vicarage Primary School, East Ham

# The Mummy Is Coming

The wind was blowing rapidly as a boy named Ben was heading to a haunted, creepy house. When he entered the place, a mad mummy jumped up and screamed at him, "You can run but do not dare hide!"

The mummy ran after the boy for hours and hours. After some time, they were talking for a while. The mummy told the little boy loudly, "I'm taking you to ancient Egypt and leaving you there because I don't like you."

The boy didn't want to explore and didn't want to live there. So the little boy said, "No you can't..."

**Amelia Zielinska (8)**
Vicarage Primary School, East Ham

# Anne Frank During The Second World War

One scary, pitch-black night, Anne was lying in her bed hoping she would fall asleep. Just as Anne started to feel tired, she heard a bomb shoot down so loudly it made her ears hurt. She crept silently out of her room but when she was walking down the stairs, the wooden floorboard creaked. She silently gasped. The Nazis could hear anything, even from five miles away! Anne hoped she'd survive this terrifying night.

The next morning, when Anne woke up, she felt relieved that she'd survived such a scary night. Anne grew stronger with every passing day.

**Zahra Sheeraz (10)**
Vicarage Primary School, East Ham

# Mummies Are Not Dummies

One gloomy night in Egypt, where the coffins lay, a mummy rose from the dead. It had been dead for 200 days. The mummy was covered in thick, white strings which looked like tissue rolls. It stretched its arms out, stood up and walked out of the pyramid. The soldiers were astonished by the mummy walking out. The two soldiers immediately turned into mummies. They started to go around the world. On their way, they made everyone into mummies. They went to Queen Seheth. They didn't get scared. Would the Earth be back to normal or would mummies live forever?

**Dakshaa Rachana Shourie Mannava (9)**
Vicarage Primary School, East Ham

# Death Awaits

It is the year 1650 and King Henry VIII is looking for his seventh wife. He sent his soldiers to look for a maiden willing to take this deadly opportunity.
After interviewing hundreds, he decided to marry a woman who was as beautiful as a blossoming spring garden. She was perfect.
The next day was their wedding day and they were really excited. Little did Henry know that something awaited him.
The day after, his wife murdered him as revenge for what he'd done to all his previous wives. Henry VIII had been stabbed in the back, literally!

**Arissa Baloch (10)**
Vicarage Primary School, East Ham

# Ancient Egypt

Today I went to ancient Egypt. As I walked across the sand, I saw pyramids and tombs placed on the desert. I saw scribes passing by pyramids, writing about them. A pharaoh sat at the top of the pyramids and ruled the whole of ancient Egypt. Sadly, the farmers who were poor had to farm at the bottom of the pyramids. Craftsmen were busy making objects so I asked them, "Hello, ancient Egyptians, can you tell me where the Nile is?" They said, "It's on the left."

When the pharaoh heard me, he offered me a walk by the Nile.

**Madeeha Iffah Hussain (8)**
Vicarage Primary School, East Ham

# The Pharaoh Of The Land

A sandstorm was approaching while the pharaoh of the land was building the Sphinx. With time running out, the pharaoh hid in a tomb but little did he know, this tomb was Tutankhamun's. He thought he had found something amazing but then *creeeaaak!* The sarcophagus had opened. The mummified body had awoken. The pharaoh screamed for help but nobody heard as he sabotaged them. With regret in his eyes, he shouted, "Mummy!"

And that was the last they heard from him. Nobody ever found his body, however, they did find his clothes...

**Hawwa Khan (10)**
Vicarage Primary School, East Ham

# GooGoo's Revenge

Once upon a time, a boy called Cursin went to the Colosseum and he saw two famous people called Devilworm and GooGoo. They fought each other as lions attacking, they were known as the two gladiators. People fought for Devilworm and he was the best. GooGoo wanted revenge as well. While it was still happening in the Colosseum, GooGoo tried to stab him but it was too late. Percy, the judge, had already said that Devilworm had the victory which meant he had won. So everyone came and cheered for Devilworm. Finally, GooGoo congratulated Devilworm happily.

**David Carian (8)**
Vicarage Primary School, East Ham

# The Great Escape From Death

Soldiers ran in the distance to the trenches as they heard the siren. The war had begun. The soldiers stood in formation, waiting for the enemies to arrive at the battlefield.

Over the horizon, the army marched down towards their trenches. Then they all went silent as the officers commanded them to attack. The soldiers charged angrily as they reached the middle of the battlefield, blood spattered the battlefield while bullets flew through the air. The soldiers completely obliterated the army until there were no soldiers left. Except for one...

**Yusuf Hussain (11)**
Vicarage Primary School, East Ham

# The Plague

"Oh, the plague! All these rats have caused it," moaned a sick woman. People were dying and doctors were wearing freaky masks. Once people had died, their family put a red cross on their doors. The streets of London were full of diseased, filthy rats. They caused diseases that spread to the people. They were coughing and sneezing all over the place. It was a sad time because people lost their beloved families. There was no cure. The only thing to do with the dead people was to chuck them into the river Thames. The whole place smelt bad.

**Kaydie Laing (9)**
Vicarage Primary School, East Ham

# The Scary Sphinx

I travelled throughout Egypt to see it and right before my eyes, there it was. The pyramid that had the head of a man and the body of an animal, the Great Sphinx. Millions were there to see the proud looking monument. We were all staring up at it when it started chasing us. We ran for our lives as it chased us.

"We're in danger," everyone shrieked. No one could understand how the immense monument came to life. All of us ran so fast that we ran out of breath. The sphinx gobbled us up.

"Yum, that was delicious!"

**Orobosa Akenzua (8)**
Vicarage Primary School, East Ham

# Sally Murphy's Grim And Gruel Day In The Orphanage

'Dear Diary,

Another day of my horrible, terrible life in the workhouse. I, Sally Murphy, have no parents and no family, so I have to survive in these tough grounds for the rest of my life. I'll talk to you about it.

When the sun breaks free my long shift begins. First, I scrub the dirty, disgusting floor. After that, I get my abominable gruel. Brutish Bill poured his gruel over my head and I got a paddling. It was another day of chores and punishments. I have to go, Matron is approaching, I'll write soon, farewell!'

**Tiffany Paito (9)**
Vicarage Primary School, East Ham

# The Boy Named Tom

There was once a boy called Tom who lived in ancient Egypt. His father was a farmer and Tom loved to swim in the river Nile, it was his favourite thing ever. His father always said to him, "Don't swim too far or you'll get lost."
One day, Tom swam really far and was lost for thirty-five years. His mother and father were terrified, they didn't know what had happened to him.
One day, the boy came back and he had a full beard now. He reunited with his family and they all lived happily ever after in their hut.

**Josephine Opoku (7)**
Vicarage Primary School, East Ham

# The Mammoths Are Coming

"Aargh!" screamed the terrified Stone Age girl as she was chased by a majestic brown mammoth. She tried to run away but the mammoth got faster and faster as it used its tusks. A few more minutes later, the brown fluffy mammoth got so tired it went away. The scared girl hid in a dark, deep cave.
An hour later, she thought it was safe to come out. She heard a mammoth howl loudly. She quickly followed the sound and she saw the mammoth on the mountain. She instantly rescued the mammoth by climbing on the steep, rocky mountain.

**Mehrin Miah (8)**
Vicarage Primary School, East Ham

# The Ottoman Soldier

There was once an Ottoman soldier who was as brave as a lion and as sly as a fox. He had many names which his tribe called him.

One day, a big battle occurred with the nearest Christian army. Fighting for their tribe, the brave soldiers made the crusaders retreat. Sadly, the brave lion was ambushed and injured. Shaking, he was taken to the arrogant commander of the Christians to be beheaded in front of everybody. However, like a sly fox, he took out a secret dagger from his pocket and stabbed the commander, leaving him for dead.

**Muhammad Yusuf Bin-Jamal (11)**
Vicarage Primary School, East Ham

# Lucy And The Dinosaur

Lucy was camping with her friends. They were playing happily and prancing everywhere. As they got tired, they wanted to go to sleep, so they did. Lucy Gene woke up from a dream and she couldn't go back to sleep. So she stayed up and she got bored. So she started to wander off. As she wandered, she got lost. She called her friends but they couldn't hear her. So she walked and saw a glowing cave. She went inside and searched everywhere. As she was searching, she heard a mighty roar. She turned around... There was a dinosaur!

**Bhagpreet Kaur (10)**
Vicarage Primary School, East Ham

# How The Soldier Saved My Life

That was when we heard it, the wailing sirens of the aircraft approaching. Gas had risen in the air as escapees rushed to the shelter. My family and I stood between scared, panic-stricken people. My heart was pounding, something was holding me back. I didn't know what it was. As I turned to my family, I was shocked to realise they weren't there. Immediately, soldiers poured out of their stations, gunshots ringing in my ears. Just then, a rough hand was wrapped around my waist. I was put in the trenches until the war ended.

**Sasha Vasudevan (11)**
Vicarage Primary School, East Ham

# The Possessed Mummy

Once there was a king and queen in Egypt who were so important. They always strolled through town.

Astonished that nothing bad had happened in town, they moved along lanes to get back home. The king was puzzled as the queen wasn't there. A few moments later, she was found bitten on a sofa. Later on that same day, the king was surrounded by his wife and a mummy. In an instant, they were splattered on the floor. He sprinted and hid behind the curtain, shouting. Surprisingly, he was found. Whoever had done it was gone!

**Oliver Ronald Otai Opolot-Oguli (9)**
Vicarage Primary School, East Ham

# The War

As I entered the war, we all got into position as quick as a flash. *Boom!* A bullet flew and fractured someone's head. The gore curdled up. We were all startled. When I looked down, the river was full of a revolting smell, it was blood! My heartbeat was fast. The captain shouted to fire and off went the dense bullets, striking the enemies. that is where the calamity rose, the penetrating noise was too much. I had to call a stretcher bearer and had to abandon the horrific war. I was so relieved, I was taken to a tent.

**Muhammad Hasnain Raza (11)**
Vicarage Primary School, East Ham

# Ancient Mummy

The sand swirled with the furious wind with a blurry vision, I headed towards my destination. My heart was pounding but I couldn't give up. As my vision got clearer, I was in disbelief. I saw a towering shadow trailing behind me. I sprinted faster and faster and faster and before I knew it, I'd collapsed and tumbled into the sandstorm. As I struggled to get up, I lifted my head and I saw an ancient mummy approaching me. As it reached out to me, I panicked and screamed. Then I realised that it was only trying to help me.

**Ayaan Zaman (10)**
Vicarage Primary School, East Ham

# A Horror Of A Fire

"Fire! Fire! Wake up, wake up now!" screamed frightened people, running down the streets as mice and rats scattered around their feet, hurrying to escape.

As they turned to look back, within a blink of an eye, the whole city was alight like an explosion. It was happening everywhere and the light was blinding, they could barely gaze as St Paul's Cathedral fell. It became more alight as the houses crashed together, making a dangerous domino effect. The fire was as hot as a dragon's furious, fiery breath...

**Charlotte Cordery (8) & Lottie Cordery (8)**
Vicarage Primary School, East Ham

# The Jewel Of Spring

There was a legend that there was a God of Spring that went crazy without the Jewel of Spring. This happened in ancient Greece.

Ava was a special girl. The girl was sent on a quest. In return, she would marry the king's son. Well, the jewel was a soft, pink colour. She obviously accepted it.

After a month, people thought she was dead, even the king. But she came back and she threw the jewel in the air and it disappeared. Spring came back! Ava and Prince Vase fell in love and married. They had a girl called Lily.

**Samira Yasmin (9)**
Vicarage Primary School, East Ham

# The Great Smell

When the government was having a meeting they started to smell a bad aroma as the sewer waste and dead bodies made such a smell. The government had to take the meeting to another area where there was no smell of the River Thames.

After, Joseph Bazalgette and all of his workers made the sewage system. They made 21001 kilometres of pipes which cleared the river and the smell went.

After that, the government went back to the Houses of Parliament and carried on their meeting, thanks to the sewage system and Bazalgette.

**Hamzah Khan (10)**
Vicarage Primary School, East Ham

# Unicorns

Once upon a time, there was a unicorn. It had rainbow hair and white, fluffy skin. Her name was Lilly and she had an owner called Amy. Since they lived on Rainbow World, they had to keep it private because Amy didn't like people around.
When Neil Armstrong went to space, he saw Rainbow Land. He didn't want to go on it yet, so Neil Armstrong decided that he would go on it on his next adventure. He alerted everyone he knew to the planet and he crept up into Amy's window to see them, not letting Amy know...

**Nafisa Mahmad (9)**
Vicarage Primary School, East Ham

# Hanging

I saw a big crowd of people, some of them were forgotten friends, nervy neighbours and snobby, rich ladies and gentlemen. I walked slowly so I could see if he was there. He wasn't there! I'd taken the blame for him and he hadn't even come.
As I reached the ladder, I walked faster. It was hard climbing up the ladder with all my petticoats on. King Henry VI was there giving me looks of disgust. I walked on the wobbly, wooden plank. I put my head through the rope. I never saw him and I would never forget.

**Kenya Sammy (11)**
Vicarage Primary School, East Ham

# Mummies Are Heading For Us!

The frightening wind was blowing and an eight-year-old girl was living in her castle. She was reading a book about ancient mummies. As she was reading, the long, twirly mummy came alive and even started to talk. The mummy looked really fun but her heart was beating strongly and her jaw froze, dropping down. He came alive to capture her and put her into his own place in Egypt. The mummy had beady brown eyes and he was wrapped in toilet paper. She wanted to know why. "It's horrible!" the girl yelled loudly.

**Melissa Rainika (8)**
Vicarage Primary School, East Ham

# Mummy Of Doom

I was exploring the hot deserts of Egypt when unexpectedly, I fell down a gaping hole and hit my head on a lever. A golden tomb rose up and out came a vicious mummy. It started chasing after me, red spiders came crawling from its body. I started to scream when suddenly, I noticed the mummy's loose bandages. As I pulled it, the mummy turned into dust and vanished. The mummy's dust went on my shoes and as I blew the dust away, I was transformed back to my bedroom. I never want to go back to Egypt ever again.

**Layla Kaur (9)**
Vicarage Primary School, East Ham

# Wooden Horse

It was a hot, sunny day and the sand was burning my feet. The walls were tall and high, there was no way we could break through. Our king had brought us an entire army but how? We weren't heroes or gods, just men. How could we possibly fight the mighty city of Troy?

"Get some wood," I shouted. "We'll make a wooden horse."

When we'd built the horse, they pulled the horse into the tower with us inside. Finally, when we entered the tower, we defeated the mighty city of Troy.

**Hannan Khalid (10)**
Vicarage Primary School, East Ham

# War Time

In the middle of the night, I woke up to a sword swooshing through my demolished window. Peering out, enormous ships now lay flattened out on the seashore as Vikings with axes devoured the remains of the forsaken ships. Charging towards my village, their bloodthirsty axes and horned helmets were too much for us.

Within a few hours, my beloved village had fallen. I overheard them telling each other to raid the houses. *Bang!* My door had come down so I looked around for somewhere to hide... But where?

**Muhammed Zaheer Hussain (10)**
Vicarage Primary School, East Ham

# The Minutes Of My Dream

I started running from the gunshots, my heart was pounding crazily. I could die if they shot me. I was breathing heavily, forcing my legs to move. The German soldiers had a lot of ammunition and I saw many British soldiers getting shot at. My family used to be the thing that gave me courage and I had courage as I thought of my family, they gave me even more courage for what I was about to do. I got my gun and went into war. I shot many Germans until I was shot.

"Those cursed Germans," I said.

**Yusuf Afnan Hussain (10)**
Vicarage Primary School, East Ham

# Rose Marshall's Time Machine

Rose Marshall, a twelve-year-old girl, loved to build new inventions. So one day, she decided to build a time machine and go back in time to Egypt. It took her days, which turned into months, to build that time machine. Finally, it was ready. She pressed the 'on' button and *pop!* She was gone in a flash. In a blink of an eye, she arrived in Egypt in 170 BC. It was just amazing! She did so much and even visited a pyramid. But soon she got fed up. She found the time machine and went home.

**Sumayyah Ahmed (10)**
Vicarage Primary School, East Ham

# The Mystery Creature

A long time ago, I was chased by a scaly animal. I ran for my life. I couldn't believe my eyes. I thought I was dreaming but then the unthinkable happened, there were more! They were like a flock of birds, there were so many of them. I thought it was the end.

I hit a dead-end and I knew I was a goner. I'd never been so scared. Then a miracle happened, there was a cave... but it was full of the vicious things chasing me. This was the end.

I know now that they were cruel, vile dinosaurs.

**Dylan Brown (9)**
Vicarage Primary School, East Ham

# Ending WWII

Two weeks ago, life wasn't easy when my friends and I were fighting during WWII. We waited in the fields for the enemies to attack. Soon they'd arrived and we attacked. There were thousands of them actually fighting. We had to defeat these disgusting, stinky enemies. But how? We could do this. Minutes later, we saw and found out that there were only half of the enemies left. So we carried on until we ended up fighting the boss. We hit him multiple times and the war came to an end. Finally.

**Muhammed Zahir Miah (10)**
Vicarage Primary School, East Ham

# Stuck In Time!

Jeff woke up from a nightmare, so he paid a visit to his friend Bob, a scientist. Bob had finished the project he'd been working on which was a time-travelling car. Jeff wanted to see if the car worked and he also wanted to see how WWI had started, for a school project. So they went there.
As soon as they got there, Jeff was happy that the car worked. So they decided to stay for a while. The next day, the car was taken by Hitler to Germany, so they stayed for WWI. Then they died in WWI.

**Shanjai Sritharan (11)**
Vicarage Primary School, East Ham

# Anne Frank

In a warm and cosy bedroom, a gorgeous girl sat down reading her diary. She was named Anne Frank. She loved mummies but not when she was sleeping. She valued school but not homework. Anne always wanted an ink pen but never had one. Anne's dream was to visit ancient Egypt but trust me, this would never happen.

Once, her beloved dad, Frank, bought her an ink pen but she was nowhere to be seen. Her mum and dad were petrified and frightened. The cops were called and blood was seen everywhere...

**Santhiya Maheswaran (11)**
Vicarage Primary School, East Ham

# The Sabre-Tooth Tiger

I got lost while shopping with my friends and ended up in a deserted jungle. Every step I made on the flamboyant, green leaves went *crunch*. Everything was green. Abruptly, lightning struck and the wind howled. A deafening roar echoed through the wild before it reached my ears. My pulse quickened. *Roar!* I jerked back. Every step it made felt like an earthquake. I was startled but the alluring sight of the meteor shower left a smile on my face. The sabre-tooth tiger smiled as well...

**Humayra Islam (11)**
Vicarage Primary School, East Ham

# Invasion!

Once upon a time, a mummy lived in a tomb for over a thousand years. One day he came back to life when the museum was about to close. The mummy decided to wait until he heard no footsteps, so he could escape and free himself. Once he was free, he went to look for the controller which he created himself and was used for the past 1000 years. He found it and set free all sorts of creatures, mainly zombies. They all greeted each other and then the alarm went off, so they knew to go back to normal.

**Areebah Butt (10)**
Vicarage Primary School, East Ham

# The Boy With Long Hair

There was a little boy who had long hair. He was in the Stone Age, so he needed to work.

One day, he went into a deep, dark wood to pick strawberries. He saw a huge monster digging. He hid behind the tree and then the monster went away with a tiny, colourful bag. The boy looked into a hole that the monster had dug. There was so much bronze. He ran and ran back to the village and told them. The villagers got the bronze and it became the Bronze Age, so they didn't need to work as much.

**Linh Pham (8)**
Vicarage Primary School, East Ham

# Creepy Woods

Once upon a spooky time, a silly, rude boy ran into the gloomy, foggy woods because everybody called him a coward. He stumbled over a tree but it wasn't a normal tree, it was a creepy, paranormal tree.

Two hours passed by as he figured out it was a haunted forest. Before he could blink, something came out. *What was it? Where had it come from? Was it the end?* There was a mummy! He found a knife and started slaying the mummy. It was Tutankhamun. Would that happen again?

**Yahya Khan (8)**
Vicarage Primary School, East Ham

# The Revenge Of The Ghost Of Sparta

In 480 BC, there was an immense war with the Spartans and Athenians. I, Kratos, was only a child when my family were hiding from the war. As I stood up like the great Leonides, Thuner killed my family. I was depressed.

Years later, I still have that night in my mind but no, I wanted to kill Thuner for good. So I got what I needed and set off. I met two new people called Freya and Atreus. They helped me find Thuner and we did. We had a battle and I hit him to the floor, not moving.

**Yasir Ali (9)**
Vicarage Primary School, East Ham

# The Story Of The Bossy Pharaoh

I travelled across Egypt, I was hungry and thirsty. I came across a pharaoh and his slaves were all working. I asked the pharaoh if he had some food and drink.

He said, "No, unless you help me."

I asked him what I needed to do and he told me to find a mummy. We made a deal.

The next day, I woke up and started my journey. I walked and I came to a hut and went inside. I was terrified but I found a box with a mummy. The mummy chased me. I went back and had food.

**Khadija Hessa Nasim (8)**

Vicarage Primary School, East Ham

# The Space Mission NASA

In the year 1969, Neil Armstrong went to space to explore the moon. At the countdown of ten, the rocket flew into space.

After flying to the moon, Neil Armstrong planted the flag and he became the first man on the moon.

After a while, Bob, the alien, went to see Neil Armstrong to be friends with him. Sadly, Neil had to go. So Neil Armstrong counted to ten and finally, went back to Earth to research his friend Bob, the nice friendly alien. Neil was really impressed and amazed.

**Muhammad Azeel (9)**
Vicarage Primary School, East Ham

# The Family And The Danes

I was abused by nobles and now I am abused by Danes. On the day of Saint Cuthbert, one thousand pagans broke into the city of York. My parents, my sister and I ran and hid. In the confusion, they hid as monks and I hid in a bush. Fifty minutes later, they were marched out to sea, never to be seen. Then I blacked out.

I saw a hairy, angry Dane. He was shouting and wearing Thor's hammer. He pointed an axe to me. I'm now a slave to the hairy, ugly, dumb, weird Danes.

**Rayan Amjad Ishaq (10)**
Vicarage Primary School, East Ham

# The War

There once was a tribe called the Anglo-Saxons and they were superb fighters. One day, there was an attack between the Anglo-Saxons and the Vikings. It was a very tough war and they thought they were doomed but suspiciously, a man appeared with a very long beard. He had a hat which looked like the Vikings' one but fiercer. He said, "Stop now, I am warning you."
"I wonder what he is going to do?" said Amy, Josh and Max together. Then they ran.

**Joylen Colaco (9)**
Vicarage Primary School, East Ham

# The Mummy Nap

I'm in a hot place where ice cream would melt. I walked in the hot sand and I saw a village with people. I felt a shadow above my head. I looked behind me and a mummy monster was looking at me. It had big green eyes.

"Who are you?" I called but he growled. I screamed loudly as if I had a microphone. I ran as quick as a flash to a bush. I looked around and heard the mummy. I got two sticks and started to unwrap them and there was a pile of bones...

**Anaya Sharma (8)**
Vicarage Primary School, East Ham

# The Adventure Of Hazel Jane

Hello, I'm Hazel Jane and I want to tell you about the adventure I had when I found the rare emerald-green venomous dragon! Let me tell you about it: I packed my suitcase and left. I was so anxious that I started to regret doing it but I said to myself, "No, you have to do this!" So I set off in my plane and it was exhausting but I didn't give up. I finally found it. It had luscious green wings and a scaly body. I was speechless. I loved it.

**Shemoli Harrus (10)**
Vicarage Primary School, East Ham

# How To Survive Vikings

Living in northern Europe isn't fun for the Vikings. One day, I was walking when a boat came out of the river. It had an animal and some shields, I knew that they were the Vikings. I made a decision to run away but it was such a bad idea as they chased me. I ran as fast as I could but still, they chased me. When I lost them I found a hiding place but one found me. I couldn't escape, so I gave him some gold and he went back to the boat. Gone, forever.

**Arafathzaman Mohamed**

Vicarage Primary School, East Ham

# A Horror Of Florence Nightingale

On Monday 29th July 1699, everyone was asleep but that night, Florence Nightingale went to work. She had to leave her husband and children. They lived in a bakery on Pudding Lane. Their dad was a baker and Florence was a nurse. When Florence was away, the dad asked his son to close the oven door. The son was so tired that he forgot to close it. So the rocks fell and burnt the houses.

"Fire, fire! Everyone, wake up, there is a huge fire here!"

**Goda Matuleviciute (8)**
Vicarage Primary School, East Ham

# The Dinosaur Cave Hunt

Once there was a man whose job was to hunt dinosaurs. One day, his boss said that he had a mission and to complete it, he had to find the dinosaur cave and he had to get all the bones. So the man went off and followed the steps. He found that they were shaped like a dinosaur. Soon he found the cave and it was dark and deep. Then he found a dinosaur and quickly got himself out and ran to his boss. He got an award for finding a real dinosaur!

**Sukhleen Kaur Bains (8)**
Vicarage Primary School, East Ham

# The Beast

The wind was howling and I was dashing between the trees, trying to lose sight of the unknown and strange creature. After a few seconds of sprinting, there was a big, straight cliff in front of me. There was no way I could escape. I turned around and was face-to-face with the brute. My jaw dropped and my heart froze at the sight of the fiend. It had piercing claws with razor-sharpened teeth and scaly, patterned skin. It was a dinosaur...

**Nada Hassan (11)**
Vicarage Primary School, East Ham

# The Maxwells Versus The Johnstones

The Maxwells floundered across the battlefield. They spotted the Johnstones and charged hurriedly along towards them. The Maxwells and the Johnstones jumped off their bog-trotters and shouted 'fight'. So they began fighting violently. It was loud and very bloody. The Maxwells were nearly all dead. There were only about ten people left fighting for the clan. It was outrageous! The battle was nearly over but the men had to fight again.

"Here we go!" the Johnstones screamed. They were still fighting when the moon came up. Eerily, the bloodstained daggers glinted in the moonlight. The Johnstones had won.

**Ellis Lindores (9)**
Wilton Primary School, Hawick

# Hunted Alive

Slowly and sneakily, the caveman violently began to hunt. Suddenly, the caveman ducked down low. Something was coming... The ground vibrated. Behind the bushes, something humongous and furry appeared. It was the last woolly mammoth on Earth. Dangerously, the caveman jumped on it. They lumbered through the trees until they came to a den where there was a huge sabre-toothed tiger. "Fight," the caveman said. So they had a ferocious battle. the mammoth charged while the caveman shot an arrow. The tiger sunk his long, sharp teeth into the mammoth's throat and that's how they became extinct.

**Sophie Morozzo Della Rocca (10)**
Wilton Primary School, Hawick

# Viking Days

The Vikings quietly sailed towards northern Scotland to burn and deconstruct buildings which were weak. They also destroyed families by killing them. The most fearsome Vikings, Toke and Ultimate Thor, were both brave and strong. They raged ahead and burnt buildings, wrecking anything they saw. But the people of northern Scotland tried to defend their loved land but they didn't survive. The two Vikings threatened terror and death. Anyone who messed with them would be slain. Toke and Thor loaded all the stolen goods onto one of their longships and left the Scots with absolutely nothing.

**Lucas Harry jay Harding (9)**
Wilton Primary School, Hawick

# The Raiding Reivers

In the middle of the dark, creepy night, the Maxwells jumped out of the cobwebbed bush. They hid behind the trees in the woods outside Hawick. They heard slow, sneaky footsteps of the Johnstone clan. The Maxwells dived out and they began shouting, "Attack! Attack!"
There were puddles of blood and dead men everywhere. Even though they still wanted to carry on, they had used up all of their breath by screaming and shouting. After they realised this, the Maxwells had won. They stopped and returned to their homes. They put their feet up and relaxed until the next raid.

**Jenna Quinn (9)**
Wilton Primary School, Hawick

# The Fussy King

Suddenly there was a slicing sound and a high-pitched scream. There was silence, all throughout the town square. Henry the VIII had just killed his wife because she'd had a baby girl called Mary. Henry didn't want her because he said she looked very ugly. Soon after that, Henry married again. Soon Queen Anne was pregnant. As soon as her baby was born, Henry complained again. It was a cute baby boy, however, everybody wondered why he was complaining this time. King Henry VIII actually wanted a girl. They told him to make up his mind!

**Evie Cranston (10)**
Wilton Primary School, Hawick

# Reivers' Revenge!

Wickedly, the Rutherford clan headed straight in for the Armstrongs and were not giving up. But at the same time, the Armstrongs were suffering. Both clans were weakly still fighting on with only a couple of men down.

Sneakily, the Rutherfords were pretending to be dead on the ground. Silently and slowly, they sneaked up behind the Armstrongs and brutally stabbed them all at once. The Rutherfords were blissfully happy that they had won. It was an evil but tremendous victory. However, soon the Armstrongs would return for revenge.

**Lexi Shiell (10)**
Wilton Primary School, Hawick

# Cleopatra's Traps

*Snap!* Something clutched my foot. I didn't know what it was, so I began to panic. Then I saw the initials *CT* on the metal. At first, I thought it must be a trap buried from long ago but suddenly there was a wicked laugh. *CT* must mean Cleopatra's traps! I tried to wriggle free but while I was struggling, all of a sudden a pyramid fell on top of me. Freaking out, I walked over to a dusty tomb. I didn't want to open it just in case but I did and there were dead people!

**Aiva Zoe Barker (9)**
Wilton Primary School, Hawick

# YOUNG WRITERS INFORMATION

We hope you have enjoyed reading this book – and that you will continue to in the coming years.

If you're a young writer who enjoys reading and creative writing, or the parent of an enthusiastic poet or story writer, do visit our website www.youngwriters.co.uk. Here you will find free competitions, workshops and games, as well as recommended reads, a poetry glossary and our blog.

If you would like to order further copies of this book, or any of our other titles give us a call or visit **www.youngwriters.co.uk.**

Young Writers
Remus House
Coltsfoot Drive
Peterborough
PE2 9BF

(01733) 890066
info@youngwriters.co.uk

**f** YoungWritersUK

**y** @YoungWritersCW